I0621525

Neon

Elise Noble

Published by Undercover Publishing Limited

r10

ISBN: 978-1-910954-29-4

Edited by Nikki Mentges, NAM Editorial

Cover design by Elise Noble

www.undercover-publishing.com

www.elise-noble.com

Don't let anything dull your sparkle.

CHAPTER 1

ONE, TWO, THREE, four, five... Oh, pluck a duck, he'd lost one again. Trying to get those girls in one place was harder than herding cats. Cats with ADHD who'd been popping acid. Bradley should know—he'd been running around after them for long enough.

"Where's Carmen?"

Emmy shrugged and took another sip of coffee. "Think she went to get her Korth."

Bradley let out a long sigh. Why did he do this?

"I've already told her that she doesn't need a gun. We're going to a spa resort, not a war zone."

"Health farm," Emmy muttered, and he glared at her.

"Spa resort. *You* need to get healthier. How many cups of coffee have you had today?"

"Two."

"Three. And it's not even seven o'clock. Breakfast should be a smoothie and porridge according to Toby, not caffeine and a donut."

Over the years, Bradley had spent many hours conferring with Toby, Emmy's nutritionist. The two men shared a sense of despair when it came to encouraging Emmy and her friends to do what was good for them. Bradley loved each and every one of those girls from their pretty heads to their karate-kicking feet, but their stubborn personalities sometimes made him wish he still worked in a hair salon.

Carmen sauntered into view, carrying a knapsack and a suspiciously large case, and Bradley couldn't hold back the groan that escaped.

"What's in there?"

"Accessories."

"The kind of accessories that can put a bullet through a man's head at a thousand yards?"

"Fifteen hundred."

"You don't need a sniper rifle at Cedar Ridge. We're going for three days of rest and relaxation, and they don't have anywhere for shooting."

"Nate gave me this when we got married. Think of it as an alternative wedding ring. It stays with me."

Bradley blinked a couple of times, but that only made the tic in his eye worse.

"Fine. *Fine.* Put it in the trunk."

He still had ninety-five miles to convince her to leave it there. Or perhaps he could take it out when she wasn't looking?

One, two, three, four, five... Now Mack had disappeared, and this trip was for *her* bachelorette weekend. Okay, Plan B—he needed handcuffs, duct tape, and zip ties. But he only made it halfway back to the house before Carmen opened the rear door of her Mercedes G-Wagen.

"Bradley? What's all this stuff?"

"Tia's luggage."

"But I thought we were only going for three days?"

"We are."

He still needed to break the news to Tia that all of

her admittedly excellent packing efforts had been for nothing. Cedar Ridge operated a strict dress policy, one that didn't include five-inch stilettos or cocktail dresses, which meant she wouldn't need a thing from her six suitcases while they were in the resort building.

Carmen slammed the door in disgust and shoved her things into Emmy's car instead, cursing under her breath in Spanish as she did so. And miracle of miracles, Mack ran out of the house with yet another charging cable in her hand.

She wouldn't need that either.

One, two, three, four, five...six.

"Fandabidozi! We can leave. Finally," Bradley added under his breath. "We need to be there by nine o'clock, and we're already running twenty minutes late."

Dan looked up from her perch on the hood of the car. "Emmy's driving the Cayenne. We've got plenty of time."

Bradley patted his pocket again, just in case. Yes, his Valium was still tucked safely inside. For years, he'd simply closed his eyes whenever he rode in a vehicle with Emmy, but every time she braked hard, they popped open all of their own accord. *Because it's better to see death coming.* With pharmaceutical help, he could keep his heart rate under one-forty.

"Who's with me?" Emmy asked.

"Mack's in the front, seeing as it's her party. I'll ride in the back with Dan."

Oh, how Bradley wished he could ride in Carmen's car. But Emmy would arrive first—she always did—and he needed to be there to facilitate check-in.

"Wait, wait! I forgot my sunglasses." Tia leapt out of

the car before anyone could stop her and ran towards the house.

"You have two pairs right here," Emmy yelled after her.

"Neither of those match my new swimsuit."

Deep breaths. Think happy, calming thoughts.

"Should I go and get her?" Lara offered, already climbing out of the G-Wagen.

"Thank you, Lara, but I'll go." Because otherwise two girls would be missing. "You stay here and don't let anybody else leave. Under *any* circumstances."

"What if we get attacked by aliens?" Emmy asked.

Dan giggled. Had she been drinking this morning? "Or killer monkeys?"

"I'm sure Carmen has a gun for that. *Stay here.*"

Ten minutes later, Bradley settled in for ninety-five miles of hell. As Emmy accelerated down the driveway, he checked his seat belt, checked it again, then leaned back to practise his breathing exercises.

In on three, out on five.

In on three, out on five.

Quite frankly, it was a miracle they were going to Cedar Ridge at all. The weekend had been a nightmare to arrange. Emmy, Dan, and Mack worked full-time for Blackwood, a private security firm owned by Emmy, her husband, Carmen's husband, and Lara's boyfriend. Carmen worked there part-time around being a mom. Lara volunteered for several local charities, and Tia assisted Bradley, mostly by shopping. A girl after his own heart. Their hectic schedules meant that this was the only weekend before Mack's wedding that all six of them were free, and with Luke and his bachelor party heading to Vegas at the same time, Emmy hadn't wanted to leave the office. Thankfully, Mack had resorted to blackmail.

"Ems, I'll only ever have one bachelorette party, and it won't be the same without you there."

"But what if there's an emergency?"

"The Sundown Spa is only a couple of hours away, and we'll have our phones. Plus I can access the entire Blackwood network remotely."

"We've never been away at the same time as the guys before."

"Logan said he'd stay at the office for the whole weekend, and Xav's offered to help out too."

"But—"

"If you don't come, I'm never erasing a speeding ticket for you again."

That last threat worked, and Bradley had spent weeks organising Mack's trip, only for disaster to strike at the last minute. When an early morning phone call had turned his perfectly ordered world upside down last week, he'd been on the verge of tearing out his highlights. The mere memory of it made him break out in a cold sweat...

"Is this Bradley? It's Valeria from the Sundown Spa."

Located near Blacksburg, the Sundown Spa had every amenity a person could imagine and some Bradley had never even dreamed of. A hot stone massage using actual meteorites? An ambergris and opal facial? Bradley had been tempted by the latter until he googled what ambergris was. No amount of revitalisation was worth putting *that* on his delicate visage. But sperm whale goop or no sperm whale goop, the Sundown Spa was the place to go for a weekend break.

Emphasis on the "was."

"Yes, this is Bradley. Are you calling about the goody bags? Because if there's still a supply problem with the Chateau Miel Grandé Glow cream, then a substitute would be acceptable."

"It's not about the cream." The tremor in Valeria's voice made Bradley's pulse kick up a notch, and his smartwatch began beeping at him. "There's been a small mishap."

"What kind of a mishap?"

"A therapy goat got loose in the meditation temple, and unfortunately, one of our guests had lit half a dozen mango and patchouli candles to help rebalance her chakras. One of them got knocked into the drapes, and... The fire department did a wonderful job, but I'm afraid there's no way we'll be ready to reopen in time for your friend's bachelorette celebration."

In on three, out on five.

In on three, out on five.

"How about I send a team of builders to help out?"

He didn't like Valeria's nervous giggle. "I'm afraid it's a little beyond that. Half of the main building got damaged, most of the roof fell down, and you can smell burned incense from half a mile away. But I could email a list of other spas in the area that might be able to accommodate you?"

Bradley forced a smile onto his face, even though he wanted to throw something. Not the crystal horse sculpture on the table in front of him, and not his bespoke diamond-studded clipboard either. Something else.

"That's very kind of you."

In on three, out on five.

In on three, out on five.

Screw it. He threw the phone.

Out of all the other spas he tried, only Cedar Ridge had seven rooms available at such short notice. Okay, not available, exactly, but when he begged Nate to hack into the booking system, he'd found a group of women planning a school reunion who were open to bribery. Five hundred bucks each. Not bad—he'd have paid triple if they'd pushed.

The only problem? Cedar Ridge was no Sundown Spa.

So, now Bradley and his band of badass bitches were on their way for a...well, it promised to be an interesting weekend.

While the Sundown Spa offered every modern convenience available, from the in-room cappuccino machines to Wi-Fi by the relaxation pool, Cedar Ridge promised a more holistic experience. Back to basics, at one with nature, that sort of thing.

He'd considered explaining that to the girls, really he had, but the right moment never quite came up. In truth, he'd worried that they might refuse to go at all, and they needed this break even if they wouldn't admit it. Which was why he'd taken the sensible option and simply omitted to tell them about the teensy change in plans.

They'd thank him eventually.

They would.

Right?

CHAPTER 2

"ARE YOU SURE this is the right place?" Emmy asked. "It looks kind of...primitive."

Bradley swallowed hard. His stomach had shot into his throat when Emmy slammed on the brakes, and it didn't want to go back where it belonged.

"Yes, this is the right place."

"I guess the scenery's pretty," Dan said.

Bradley nodded enthusiastically, keeping his fingers crossed that her good mood held. The scenery *was* spectacular, although the hilly vista would have been even lovelier to look at if Emmy hadn't blasted through it at eighty-five miles an hour.

As she turned into the winding driveway that led to Cedar Ridge, majestic oaks rose high on either side, wind whispering through their leaves. In the distance, a stand of cedar trees clung to the steep ridge that gave the resort its name. Bradley rolled down his window and took a bracing breath. With little traffic and no pollution, even the air smelled fresher here.

Around another bend, a cluster of low buildings sprawled in front of them, wood-sided with shingle roofs. An impressive flight of stone steps led up to the largest of them. Picture perfect, just like the brochure promised. A sign over the main door invited them into reception while a smaller arrow pointed towards the parking lot along a track to the side.

Emmy pulled into a space at the far end, and Bradley checked the GPS.

"Congratulations, you beat Carmen by fifteen minutes. Now we have to wait."

"Let's get our room keys. She'll be here by then."

Mack hopped out of the passenger side and glanced at her phone. "There's no Wi-Fi signal."

Emmy slammed the door shut. "Maybe it only works around the buildings?"

Should Bradley come clean yet? On balance, it seemed like a good idea. Better here than having Mack yell at him in reception, anyway.

"Uh, there isn't a signal anywhere."

Mack turned towards him, already a shade paler than normal, which was to say ghostly.

"What do you mean, there's no signal?"

"Internet access is banned at Cedar Ridge. The owners believe time spent without technology allows your mind and body to rejuvenate."

That was their motto—"relax your mind, rejuvenate your body, heal your soul."

"I-i-it's what?" Mack hugged her laptop case to her chest like a shield. "But I need my computer. And my phone. And my tablet. And my camera. And my e-reader. And..."

Dan put an arm around her. "It'll be okay. Stay calm. Bradley, what were you thinking?"

"Mack's been getting headaches lately. Taking a break from the screen will be good for her."

"I-I-I can't."

Dan gave Mack's hand an encouraging squeeze. "We'll all be here for you."

"What if there's a problem at Blackwood?" Emmy asked Bradley. "The control room won't be able to get hold of us."

Well, at least nobody had hit him yet.

"I gave Xav the number for reception, and the staff will relay any messages."

Mack glared, and if looks could kill...

"This is meant to be my bachelorette party. *Party*. You know, fun? I only wanted to go to the Sundown Spa because it had a VR tranquillity experience and superfast broadband all the way around the jogging trail."

"It's not my fault it burned down. Would you rather have stayed at home?"

"Yes."

Emmy took Mack's other hand. "We'll get through this together. It can't be worse than that time we went on a jungle survival training exercise and the satellite phone broke. At least we don't have to trek sixty kilometres back to civilisation. Let's go inside and get a nice cup of coffee to relax, okay?"

"Uh, there's no coffee," Bradley confessed.

Emmy's eyes lasered in on him. "For a moment there, I thought you said there wasn't any coffee?"

"Caffeine's banned here. It disrupts your sleeping pattern."

"Of course it does. That's the whole fucking point. Come on, we're going home. Mack, are you riding in the front again?"

Bradley plastered himself against the car door, holding it shut. "Nobody's going home. We're going to stroll into the hotel, laze around by the pool, get massages, and relax until Sunday."

"Caffeine helps me to relax."

"No, it doesn't."

Dan blocked Emmy before she could lift him out of the way. "Ems, it's three days. If I've got to go without sex for the whole weekend, then you can live without coffee."

Bradley plastered on a grin he didn't feel. "There, that's the spirit. Come on, it won't be as bad as you think."

Emmy folded her arms. "No, it'll be worse."

Luckily, Carmen's arrival saved Bradley from Emmy's wrath. The G-Wagen drew to a halt next to Emmy's borrowed Cayenne, and Carmen, Lara, and Tia jumped out.

"You waited?" Carmen said. "I thought you'd have gone inside."

Mack wrapped her arms even more tightly around her laptop. "We haven't, because Bradley's brought us to the modern-day equivalent of a concentration camp."

"There's no Wi-Fi," Dan explained.

Carmen's jaw dropped. "Bradley, how could you do that to Mack?"

"Because she needs a break. We all need a break."

Tia stepped forward, the voice of reason. "We don't need Wi-Fi. There're plenty of other things we can do out here in the wilderness. Why don't we dress up and have a nice posh dinner?"

"Yes, about that," Bradley mumbled. "There's kind of a dress code."

"What, like smart-casual? Black tie?"

"More like a uniform, to symbolise that everyone's equal underneath their daily facade."

"Did you get that from the fucking brochure?" Emmy asked. "Have you been indoctrinated?"

"Look, I'm not a fan of that rule either."

Emmy let out a long, slow breath. "So, is that it? No gadgets, no caffeine, no fancy clothes?"

"Almost." He cut his eyes towards Carmen. "No guns either."

"Because otherwise one of us might be tempted to shoot you," Mack muttered.

"And no dessert."

There was a sharp intake of breath from Lara, but she quickly clapped a hand over her mouth.

"It's okay, I'm good. I'm sure it'll be lovely."

Bradley led the way to the main building, skirting around a cloud of midges gathered under the overhanging trees. Truth be told, this whole back-to-nature thing wasn't for him, what with its puddles and mud and rain and heat. Give him Emmy's Amex card and a shopping mall any day.

"I'd rather be in Iraq," she muttered.

"Three days," he said. "Seventy-two hours. That's all. You never know—you might even enjoy yourselves."

Right after the devil took up downhill skiing.

CHAPTER 3

"I CAN'T BELIEVE I have to spend three days wearing bleached-out surgical scrubs," Tia complained.

Emmy plucked at the cream cotton. "It's more like a judo suit. All we need are some mats, and we could—"

"No!" Bradley held up a hand. "No physical violence."

He had to admit they were both right, though. The garments they'd been forced to wear were possibly the most hideous outfits he'd ever seen, and considering his friend Ishmael had made a dress out of cabbage leaves for his spring fashion show the year before last, that was saying something. At least today's attire didn't smell so bad.

"I still can't believe they confiscated my laptop," Mack said, wiping an eye with the back of her hand.

Bradley pulled it away from her face and gave her fingers a comforting squeeze. "They promised to lock it away securely, and you'll get it back on Sunday evening."

The nasty witch of a manager had droned on and on about the importance of a totally natural lifestyle and tried to take his diamond earrings too, citing the "no jewellery apart from wedding rings" rule. Luckily, Emmy had put her foot down and he got to keep them.

But now Emmy huffed and folded her arms. "So,

what are we doing first?"

Luckily, Bradley had memorised the first activity before the staff took his smartpad. "I thought we'd try spending an hour by the celestial flotation pool."

"We won't flipping know if we've spent an hour, will we?" Mack said.

She'd been in danger of hyperventilating when the manager confiscated her email-enabled watch as well. Or her last lifeline, as she called it. Apparently, Cedar Ridge didn't believe in the concept of time either. At least Bradley had managed to snag both sets of car keys, although he'd need to hide them carefully because he didn't trust any of the girls not to take off for the nearest town as soon as he turned his back.

"It doesn't matter if we spend more than an hour. This is your weekend to relax, so you can spend the whole day by the pool if you want to."

"I don't want to."

"Try it. Please?"

Her lip wobbled. "Fine. But if I do this, I'm bringing my tablet to the wedding reception."

Another battle of theirs, but Bradley knew how to compromise. "Okay, as long as you keep it out of sight under the table."

Their rooms lay next to each other at the back of the main building, seven doubles with a view of the swimming pool and the forest beyond. Bradley closed his eyes as he slotted his key into the lock. *Please, let them be the five-stars the brochure promised, or a decent four at least.* He swung the door wide and gingerly cracked open an eyelid. Phew. Not as awful as he'd feared.

No TV, no sound system, no minibar, and the blow-dryer was underpowered, but thankfully management hadn't eschewed the benefits of AC. Colourful art decorated the walls, the carpet was so thick his feet sank into it, and the bed was top notch with plenty of pillows.

Maybe, just maybe, this weekend wouldn't be so bad?

Or maybe it would. As Bradley shuffled along the corridor in his regulation beige flip-flops, he was thankful for the "no cameras" policy. If anyone saw him wearing this...this abomination of a robe, he'd never live it down. Ugh. Hadn't the management ever heard of tailoring?

The girls beat him to the pool, probably because he'd stopped to do his hair, and they'd bagged seven loungers in a line before stripping down to their bikinis. Well, a one-piece for Lara. Bradley still needed to work on her confidence—she had a figure that most women would die for, and most men too. Like the jerk in a Cedar Ridge polo shirt polishing tiles on the far side of the water who kept sneaking glances in her direction. If he didn't pack that in, then Bradley would need to get Emmy to have a word.

"How are your rooms?" he asked, dropping his fluffy towel onto the end seat.

"Lovely, thank you," Lara said.

Emmy glanced over. "Three escape routes—door, windows, and the AC duct near the ceiling. The lock's shit, but the lamp on the nightstand would make a decent weapon in an emergency."

"Glad you like it."

"Now what?" Dan asked. "We just sit here listening to... What is this weird music?"

"According to the website, they use brainwave entrainment stimuli to alter your brain state and help you relax."

"I'm not sure I love that idea."

"It's better than using dance music to alter your hearing ability, which is what you do every Saturday night."

Dan glowered at him before closing her eyes, and he settled back, safe in the knowledge that he was right.

The pool was beautiful—the brochure hadn't lied about that. Twelve stone columns ringed the water, the signs of the zodiac painted between them, and overhead, constellations shimmered in an otherwise dark galaxy. The comforting aroma of lavender flowed from oil burners dotted among the decorative foliage.

An hour passed, perhaps two, and all the girls fell asleep except for Emmy. She'd slipped into the pool, and now she was floating around on her back with her eyes open. Thank goodness. If she drifted off and went on one of her unconscious jaunts, everyone would be in trouble. Emmy had a terrible habit of trying to murder people in her sleep.

Bradley kept yawning, but try as he might, his mind wouldn't still. Something wasn't right. He couldn't put his finger on it at first, but all of a sudden, it came to him. Cucumber! He needed cucumber. Not to eat because it literally tasted of nothing, but for his eyes. Otherwise they'd go puffy, and Cedar Ridge had banned make-up too.

Careful not to wake the girls, he slipped his feet into

the hideous flip-flops and crept off to find a member of staff. The tile guy had disappeared when Lara covered up, and nobody had so much as offered them drinks since. Zero stars for service.

With hindsight, he should have joined Emmy in the pool instead. Where was the lobby? Every pale green hallway looked the same, his left flip-flop was chafing, and the ugly pants kept getting stuck in his ass crack. After forever and a day, he spotted a lady in a Cedar Ridge tunic and waved her down.

"Cucumber. Please, I need cucumber."

"Nutritionally balanced snacks are available in the dining room."

"It's for my eyes. Unless you have a chilled gel mask I can use?"

Honestly, with the look she gave, you'd think he'd asked for a gold-plated pot of Crème de la Mer rather than a sliced vegetable, but she did grudgingly agree to see what she could do. What seemed like an hour passed before he finally made his way back to the relaxation pool with cucumber chunks rather than slices. What did they think he wanted to do, put it in a sandwich? Good luck with that, because bread was banned too. Next time, he'd ask for a whole cucumber and get Emmy to slice it. Oh, she said she'd left her weapons behind, but Bradley would bet his favourite cashmere sweater that she had a knife somewhere in her luggage.

Hmm, was he going in the right direction this time? He paused in a hallway, sniffing the air like a hound, hoping for a hint of the lavender. Left or right?

The dilemma was solved when an angry voice cut through the air.

"Hey! Get the fuck off me."

Oh, sweet mother of Gucci, was that Emmy? He ran in her direction, cursing the flip-flops with every step. What had she done now?

As Bradley rounded the corner into the relaxation area, he wanted to sink through the marble floor. Emmy was in the pool, splashing as she fought off the tile guy, who was trying to shove her arms into a rubber ring. Every time she made a grab for him, he slipped out of her grasp until Dan, Mack, and Carmen jumped in to help.

"Don't drown him!" Bradley shrieked, but of course Emmy paid no notice whatsoever.

The girls grabbed one limb each, and between them, they managed to haul the man out of the pool. Quick as a flash, Emmy straddled him. Probably made the guy's day.

"What the fuck were you doing?"

Tile Guy coughed and spluttered as he tried to get his breath back. "I thought you were in trouble, floating in the pool like that."

Bradley marched up to him. "It's a flotation pool. That's what she's supposed to do."

"Not face down, she isn't. And she wasn't moving either."

"Emmy, is this true?"

"I was bored, okay? I thought I'd see how long I could hold my breath."

"I don't think you're meant to do that here."

She pointed at the wall. "The sign says no eating, no chanting, no yoga, and no nudity. It says nothing about breathing."

In on three, out on five.

"She's very sorry, and I promise this won't happen again. Emmy, let the man up."

The man scrambled to his feet, dripping. Tia handed Emmy a towel while Bradley offered his own to the hapless employee. No great loss. They were made from natural fibres, and if the builders at Xav's house ran out of sandpaper, those towels would make a good substitute.

"Maybe we could try a different activity?" Bradley suggested. "What else is there to do today?"

"Uh..." The tile guy took a couple of paces back from Emmy's withering glare. "What about something more physical? A session with one of our personal trainers?"

"Excellent. Be a doll and set it up, would you?"

The man practically ran out of the door.

CHAPTER 4

"THIS IS GÜNTER," Tile Guy announced after Bradley and the girls had enjoyed a light lunch of sushi and salad. "He's got a fun, boot-camp-style cardio workout lined up for you this afternoon. Have a great time!"

Emmy, Mack, Dan, and Carmen lined up on the lawn in matching black sportswear as Günter cracked his knuckles. Bradley wasn't sure whom to feel the sorriest for.

"All right, ladies—let's see what you've got."

The big man set off at a run, arms and legs pumping. Emmy rolled her eyes and led the team off after him as Tile Guy turned to Bradley and dropped his voice to a whisper.

"Günter was in the German army—he's the toughest trainer we've got. I thought the girls might appreciate that."

Emmy's regular trainer was ex-Russian special forces. Who was tougher? Bradley figured they were about to find out.

"I'm sure they'll enjoy themselves."

"Do you think they'll be okay?" Lara asked. "That trainer looked scary."

She and Tia had cried off the exercise, citing a lack of coordination and a sprained ankle respectively. Funny how Tia's limp healed itself as soon as Tile Guy wandered out of sight.

"They'll be fine. At least if they're tired, they might not complain as much. Why don't we sunbathe in the Zen garden until they get back?"

"Great idea," Tia said. "But I'm going to get a book from the library first. Anyone want to join me?"

Bradley lost track of time again, but by the time he wiped away a tear at the end of his favourite scene in *Pride and Prejudice,* the light was beginning to fade, and he realised Emmy and the girls still hadn't come back. Where were they? Was it normal for a training session to last so long? He reached for his phone to give his boss a call, then realised he couldn't because of Cedar Ridge's stupid rules. Should he ask at reception for help? Did Günter carry a phone?

"Where are the others?" Tia asked, opening her eyes and stretching her arms over her head.

"I don't know." He glanced at his empty wrist out of habit. "Do you think we should look for them?"

"Don't worry—Emmy'll be fine."

"But it's getting dark."

"So? Emmy's half vampire."

"I'm not sure..." he started, then closed his mouth as five heads came into view at the end of the lawn.

Günter dragged his feet as Emmy and Dan half-carried him across the grounds. Crickets on a cracker, what happened? Mack and Carmen didn't seem too concerned as they ambled along behind chatting.

Bradley leapt to his feet. "What did you do to him?"

Dan dropped Günter and held up both hands. "This is totally not our fault."

"You destroyed a commando."

"He did most of it himself," Emmy said. "First, he

went off at a speed he couldn't handle, and then he got lost. We tried to tell him he was going in the wrong direction, but he wouldn't listen."

"And he tweaked a back muscle doing burpees," Dan added.

Günter groaned, then stumbled over to a decorative maple tree and threw up.

Bradley put his hands on his hips. "How am I supposed to explain this to the manager?"

Carmen patted him on the arm. "I'm sure you'll think of something. Is it time for dinner yet? I'm starving."

Why him? Bradley looked over at the exhausted trainer, now kneeling on the grass, and steeled himself for another difficult conversation with the resort manager—his second of the day. The woman hadn't been too impressed with Emmy's swimming pool stunt either. What had he done to deserve this?

"This isn't food." Carmen poked at a broccoli spear with her fork. "Everything's green."

"All our food is prepared by a nutritionist, ma'am," a passing waiter told her.

"It's healthy," Bradley said. "Eating a balanced diet is important, and you've lived on tacos for the last week. Don't think I didn't notice the deliveries to the office every lunchtime."

It was actually Toby who'd noticed, but Carmen wasn't to know that. And the staff at Blackwood worked as a team.

"How are we supposed to survive on this? Do you

know how many calories we burned carrying Günter this afternoon?"

"In that case, you can have two portions of organic quinoa."

"Sometimes I hate you."

"I'm sure Toby will be happy to hear that. It means I'm doing his job right."

To Bradley's great relief, the girls ate the rest of their meals without complaining, even the zucchini noodles, which were surprisingly tasty. But what was there to do for the rest of the evening? One drawback of Cedar Ridge was the lack of nightlife. The Sundown Spa offered a movie theatre, ballroom dancing lessons, and moonlit forest walks, but Cedar Ridge closed down right after dinner, leaving the guests to hang out in the library or chat over organic fruit tea.

"Anybody want to play Scrabble?" he asked. The pamphlet in his room said there were board games in the lounge.

Emmy pushed her chair back and yawned. "Actually, I think I'm gonna head for bed. That run earlier tired me out."

A little surprising, but at least that saved Bradley from losing to a triple word score like he usually did. What about the others? Lara was practically a dictionary, and she usually loved Scrabble.

"Are you *all* going back to your rooms?"

A chorus of nods and yeses came.

"I'm going to read," Mack announced.

Great—that meant Bradley could start the copy of *Sense and Sensibility* he'd borrowed earlier as well as planning out the activities for tomorrow. Somebody needed to keep the girls occupied.

Bradley stared at the grid he'd drawn out with names across the top and activities down the side. After a quick chat with the receptionist, he'd block-booked a life coach, a tennis instructor, a beautician, and a massage therapist for tomorrow, but no matter how many times he reshuffled, he couldn't fit all the activities in. Would Lara prefer tennis or a pedicure? That one was easy. A pedicure. But he wasn't sure whether Tia would choose a massage over a manicure.

What time was it? Honestly, this lack of clocks was a joke, and he was tempted to sneak back to the car and retrieve his phone. No, no, he couldn't. Not when he'd insisted on everyone else going incommunicado for three days. It wouldn't be fair.

There was nothing else for it—he'd have to pop next door and ask Tia. Surely she wouldn't mind being woken up for something so important?

Bradley pulled on his bathrobe and gave the flip-flops a dirty look as he tiptoed barefoot into the hallway. Tia first, then he'd check whether Dan wanted to play tennis or get a facial.

Except when he knocked on Tia's door, she didn't answer. He tried again, harder, but still nothing, even when he called her name. It was the same with Dan. Silence.

Dan had always been a light sleeper, so that left him worried. And the fear only intensified when Carmen, Lara, and Mack didn't answer either. Where were they? His heart beat faster as he realised he had no choice but to try Emmy. Waking his boss was like prodding Satan with a pointy stick.

He knocked quietly, half hoping she wouldn't answer, but a minute later the door cracked open an inch and her eye appeared in the gap.

"Yes?"

"I can't wake any of the others. It's as if they're not there."

"Oh." Emmy pressed her lips together. "That's because they're in here."

"Why? I thought you were going to bed. Are you having fun and you didn't invite me?" That hurt. It really hurt. These girls were his best friends, and they'd left him out of their plans? He gave a little sniffle, then... "Hold on... Why does your room smell like cheeseburger?"

"Shit."

Bradley shoved the door and found the rest of the girls sitting on the floor, the remains of the non-sanctioned meal they'd just shared on the floor between them. His eyes narrowed.

"Where did you get that?"

"The food fairy came."

"Emmy..."

"Okay, okay. Me and Mack jogged to the diner. We saw it in the distance when Günter got us lost today."

"I can't believe you did this. One weekend, that's all you had to behave for."

And worse, they hadn't saved him any fries. Or cheesecake. And was that chocolate on the corner of Lara's mouth?

"It's no big deal."

"Yes, it is. Give me your cash and all your credit cards."

"Lighten up. It was only a few snacks."

He put a hand out, palm up. "Now."

Sulkily, the girls handed everything over. Emmy's black Amex, Dan's platinum, and the rest. They'd brought thirty thousand dollars in cash between them. Holy shiitake mushrooms.

"I'm keeping these until we get home. We've got two more days left, and you're going to behave because otherwise I'll ban Mrs. Fairfax from making her chocolate fudge cake ever again."

Mrs. Fairfax, Emmy's housekeeper, made the best cakes ever, and the threat did its job. Five girls shuffled off to their rooms as he gave Emmy one last glare and slammed the door.

Those damn girls... He loved them even when they drove him crazy.

CHAPTER 5

ON SATURDAY MORNING, the girls picked at their breakfast—hardly surprising when one considered what they'd eaten the night before.

"Where's Dan?" Bradley asked, tilting his head towards the empty seat as he stirred his organic yogurt. The buffet table offered four different flavours, and every single one of them tasted disgusting.

"She went jogging. Something about getting down with nature," Emmy said.

Well, at least one of them had seen the error of her ways. After all, the calming environment with its forests and streams was the main reason they'd come to Cedar Ridge in the first place.

And Dan's jaunt looked to have worked too, because when she sauntered in towards the end of the meal, she wore a relaxed smile with her drab cotton outfit.

"Good run?" Bradley asked.

"The best."

"Did you go far?"

"Nope. Just as far as the hot lumberjack we saw while we were out with Günter yesterday. Turns out he *is* single."

Oh, Dan. "Tell me you didn't...?"

"Too damn fucking right I did. Twice. We're

supposed to be here to relax, right? And what better way to relax than getting pounded against a tree?"

A middle-aged lady at the next table spat a mouthful of peppermint tea all over the white tablecloth, and Bradley leapt in with a handful of napkins, full of apologies.

"I'm so sorry about my friend—she's only joking."

"No, she isn't," Emmy said, grinning. She wound people up for sport.

"Shh, be quiet," Bradley hissed, preparing himself to apologise to the manager yet again. "You've got a life-coaching session in half an hour, and I don't want to hear another word from you until then."

"Life-coaching?"

"Yes, and you're darn well going to enjoy it."

"What the hell is life-coaching? I've already got enough trainers at home."

"The coach will help you to identify and achieve your goals. He's meant to be excellent."

"My goal is to have pizza for dinner this evening. What's he going to do? Lend me twenty bucks and drive me to the restaurant?"

"Please, just try it. For Mack's sake."

Mack looked up from the porridge she'd been staring at for the past ten minutes. "I'm with Emmy on the pizza."

A miracle happened, and Bradley only needed to apologise once more before lunch. Dan and Carmen had gotten a tad too enthusiastic in their tennis match and bruised the coach's ego as well as his genitals.

After a woefully inadequate meal of egg-white omelette with asparagus, a pretty masseuse soothed away his aches and pains before dinner. The girls were getting facials, although no amount of cleansing and toning could get rid of Emmy's scowl. At least Tia had a smile on her face as they sat down to eat.

"What the hell is this?" Emmy poked at the whitish lumps on her plate. "Tofu?"

Dan popped a forkful into her mouth. "Doesn't taste of anything, so probably."

"On the bright side, we've only got one more day here, and my nails look great," Tia said, holding out a hand. And yes, the beautician had done a splendiferous job on her manicure. Tia had gone for the gothic look with dark red polish and black tips.

"Emmy, you should get yours done like that," Dan said. "They're perfect for the wicked queen."

"How?" Emmy dropped her cutlery onto the plate and held out one hand. "I've gone more than twenty-four hours without coffee. Look at me—I'm bloody shaking. I'd end up with the polish all over my fingers."

Wow, yes, she actually was. Good thing she didn't have to shoot anyone today.

"You never used to be this addicted," Bradley told her. "Since the whole Colombian episode, you've been drinking far too much of the stuff."

"Eduardo bought a coffee plantation, and he keeps sending me samples."

"At least he isn't sending you his other products."

Eduardo was one of Colombia's primo drug lords. Bradley had never met him, but he had to concede that the man had excellent taste. He gifted Emmy beautiful jewellery, and last year, he'd bought her a pair of matching gold-plated revolvers.

"I just need a coffee, okay?"

"No, you need to cut down on caffeine, and going cold turkey is the best way. Mack, how's your headache?"

"It's a little better."

"That's because you haven't spent the last two days staring at a screen. We all know that Dan didn't manage to abstain from her favourite vice, but going without a gun for forty-eight hours hasn't killed Carmen, has it?"

"No," Carmen conceded. "But for every day I spend away from the range, my accuracy drops by a millimetre. That could mean the difference between life and death."

"Now you're just being melodramatic. And Tia's survived in these awful clothes."

Tia held the fabric away from her neck and grimaced. "At least you admit they're horrible now."

"Plus Lara's done okay without eating dessert."

In fact, Lara hadn't eaten much at all. Today's vegetables were a tiny bit bland, so Bradley couldn't blame her for that.

Lara tried a smile, but it was shaky. "I suppose I do eat too much chocolate."

"There we go. This place is mostly good for us."

Bradley felt like the biggest fraud in Virginia as he changed into his new Versace jeans and a cashmere sweater. A quiet moan escaped his lips as its softness embraced him. Despite his earlier words to the girls, he hated Cedar Ridge and its regimented rules. How could people live this way? It was like being in the dark ages. Ah, his silver cowboy boots felt so good after those awful flip-flops. Custom made with platinum spurs on the back, they'd cost Emmy a fortune when she bought them for him last Christmas. Did she know she'd bought them? Bradley wasn't certain. Emmy might have paid attention to detail when she was at work, but she rarely checked her credit card statement, and he doubted she'd read the thank-you note he'd put in her Christmas card either.

His stomach rumbled as he fished the key to Carmen's G-Wagen out of the hollowed-out shampoo bottle he'd hidden it in. The girls laughed at him for buying spy gadgets from the internet, but who was laughing now?

Food. He needed proper food, and thankfully he'd had the forethought to pack a nice selection in case a situation like this arose. Twinkies, Reese's Peanut Butter Cups, chips, cookies, candy... His mouth was watering already.

The window squeaked a little as he raised it, and he added another check mark to Cedar Ridge's list of shortcomings. What did the maintenance team do all day? Bradley swung a leg over the windowsill, careful not to snag his jeans on any splinters, and paused to check left and right in case any of the girls happened to be taking in the starry night. Phew, the curtains in each room were tightly drawn.

"Going somewhere?" Emmy asked.

Bradley clutched at his chest. Where was she? His gaze darted among the shadows, but still he saw nothing until she stepped from behind an old maple tree, dressed in dark colours from head to toe.

"How did you get out here?"

"Used the door like any normal fucker. You didn't answer my question."

"Uh, I need to stretch my legs."

"Bullshit. You spent the whole afternoon on the massage table, and leg-stretching wasn't a problem then. Nice outfit, by the way."

"I'm allergic to those ugly tunics."

"They're made from cotton. How can you be allergic to cotton?"

"It's more the style."

"Why am I not surprised? So, where are you really going?"

Bradley sighed and leaned back against the wall. "I may have left a few snacks in Carmen's car."

"Great. Make sure you bring enough back for seven." Emmy turned and ambled towards the hotel building, whistling badly.

"Wait! What were you doing out here?"

"I was going to pick up burgers again, but now I don't have to."

"But I took all your money."

"Bradley, Bradley, Bradley. I've been at this game a lot longer than you, young grasshopper. You missed the ten grand in my bra and the credit card sewn into the back of my knickers."

"Sometimes I hate you."

"We'll be in my room. Do me a favour and hurry up —we're starving."

Rats and double rats. He needed to get better at sneaking around. Emmy caught him every time, like that day when he'd borrowed her Dodge Viper without asking and she tapped him on the shoulder as he was putting the keys back. The palpitations had gone on for hours.

Bradley kept an eye out for hotel staff as he jogged to the parking lot because the last thing he wanted was to end up in the manager's office again. That woman had a forked tongue, and she knew how to give a good lashing with it. Why had Carmen parked right at the far end? Now he'd have even farther to walk back, and the duffel bag full of snacks was heavy. Next time, he'd put the food in a suitcase instead, and then he could wheel it.

Wait a second... Next time? There would be no next time. Never again would he pay to go anywhere described as "rustic."

A creature flew past, its wings an inch from Bradley's face. A bat? Whatever it was, he jumped a foot off the ground. This place sure was creepy at night. And who had abandoned their van in such an inconvenient spot? Bradley skirted around it, but it was blocking at least three vehicles. He made a mental note to have a word with the desk staff tomorrow. Honestly, people should show some courtesy. Now, where had he put the car keys?

A quiet *crunch* made him turn, but he never found out what the sound was. Fire burst through his skull, and the pain was the last thing he remembered before the flames subsided and darkness took over.

CHAPTER 6

"WHERE THE HELL is Bradley?" Dan asked. "He's been gone for at least fifteen minutes."

Good question. How long did it take to walk to the parking lot and back? If he'd pulled a fast one and headed out for dinner, Emmy would give no quarter. Unless of course he'd gone to get tacos, in which case she might be able to find a little forgiveness in her cold black heart.

Carmen leaned back on the bed. "I bet he brought Reese's Pieces, and now he's sitting in my SUV eating them all."

Emmy pulled her watch cap back on again. "Little sod. I'm going to find him."

"Not without us, you're not," Mack said.

"Get a move on, then. I'm hungry."

The other girls put on jackets, and Tia swapped her stilettos for something more practical. Emmy waited by the door, tapping a foot as she urged them to hurry up. Sugar wasn't the only thing she was desperate for. Not only did Carmen have food in her vehicle, but she also had several sachets of instant coffee stashed in a door pocket. How did Emmy know that? Because she'd put them there. Her husband had spent a decade instilling the need to be prepared, and she'd taken his words to heart. Now she left Nescafé everywhere. *In case of emergency, add water and stir.*

"Shhh!" she told a giggling Tia as they headed out the door.

"Sorry."

As they stole towards the car park, Emmy gritted her teeth at the sound of Tia's and Lara's footsteps. Sure, they were only going to fetch Bradley, but old habits died hard, and she hated making noise. When moving in near darkness, silence was golden and shadows were your friend.

But where *was* Bradley? They got all the way to Carmen's car without seeing any sign of him, and the doors were still locked.

"Surely even Bradley couldn't have got lost on the way to the car park?"

His sense of direction was terrible, but that would be taking things to a whole new depth.

"Maybe he forgot the keys?" Dan suggested.

"Perhaps, but we'd have seen him on his way back in." And now Emmy's spidey senses were tingling. "I don't like this."

A knife found its way into her hand, a trusty Emerson CQC-7 scarred from past battles won. Hey, the bitch on reception hadn't said anything about knives, okay? Emmy could only assume that was an oversight seeing as they'd banned everything from raised voices to earbuds. She'd already flipped the blade open when rustling came from the trees on the far side of her car.

Acting on instinct, Emmy shoved Tia down behind the Porsche while Dan got Lara out of the way. Moonlight glinted off the knife in Carmen's hand—her first choice was always the Benchmade Presidio.

"Who's there?" Emmy called out.

Nothing but silence.

Emmy pointed a finger to her left, and Carmen glided in that direction, then melted into the trees. Whoever was out there, they'd flank him. Emmy mirrored Carmen to the right while the others hunkered down behind the car.

The skinny pines didn't offer much cover, but the man Emmy spotted ahead didn't so much as glance backwards. Nor did he appear to have a weapon as he clutched at the tree trunk in front of him with shaking hands.

"Boo," she whispered as she twisted his arms behind his back.

But there was no answer because Carmen quickly clamped a hand over his mouth to muffle the shriek.

The dude couldn't have weighed more than one-thirty, and when he stopped struggling, Emmy used her belt to bind his hands. Then Carmen lifted his feet while Emmy grabbed under his armpits. Yeuch. This guy was sweaty. Caused by fear or merely poor hygiene?

It was only when they got him out into the moonlight that Emmy recognised the man.

"Nigel?" She'd wasted an hour with the life coach this morning. He'd grinned and nodded enthusiastically while she lied her head off before her tennis lesson. "Why the fuck are you hiding in the woods?"

"I-I-I'm not."

Bullshit. "You expect us to believe you were taking a shortcut?"

"Uh..."

"I'll get the truth out of you eventually, so you might as well save us time and spill it now."

Nigel squinted up at her, and then his eyes widened in recognition. "Emerson? Is that you?"

"Well spotted."

His forehead creased in confusion. "But you said your life's ambition was to learn needlepoint. Why are you sneaking around the woods dressed in black?"

"It's actually dark purple, but that's an easy mistake to make in poor lighting."

"Good choice. Far better to add some colour into the mix, although black pants would work well with an eggplant top for variety."

"Thanks, I'll remember that."

"We want to know about Bradley," Carmen reminded her.

"Oh, yeah. What are you doing out here?"

"I-I-I was on my way home."

"Through the woods?"

"N-n-no. I ran into the forest when the two men leapt from behind the van and hit the gentleman walking in front of me. I guess I p-p-panicked."

Fuck, had that been Bradley?

"The man who was hit, what did he look like?"

"About my size with blond hair. I don't think he was staying here because he was wearing jeans and a sweater rather than Cedar Ridge guest attire."

Dammit. "What happened after they hit him?"

"He fell down, and they put him into the back of the van and drove off."

"And you didn't think to call for help?"

"My phone's in my car—we're not allowed them on site." Nigel gestured towards an ancient Mazda Miata.

"I was going to get it, but then I heard you coming, and I got so scared I couldn't move."

Dan took a tiny yet powerful torch out of her pocket and walked slowly along the car park before crouching, touching her fingers to the ground, and taking a sniff.

"There are scuff marks over here, plus a smear of blood."

Nigel was shaking so hard that Emmy figured the kid was telling the truth, which left the million-dollar question, or possibly more if a ransom was involved. Who the fuck took Bradley?

"Did you get the van's licence number? Can you describe the men?"

Nigel shook his head. "It was too dark. I only saw them for a second, and they were moving so fast..."

"Fuck." So much for a relaxing weekend. Although if Emmy was honest, hunting kidnappers was more fun than anything Cedar Ridge had to offer. If anyone but Bradley had been abducted, she might even enjoy the exercise. "Right, we need to fix this mess."

"You mean call the cops?"

"No, I don't mean call the sodding cops. They'd take ages to do anything, and when they did get their fingers out, they'd screw everything up."

"But what other option do we have? I'm a life coach, and you're an artist, for goodness' sake."

Dan snorted a laugh. "An artist? But you can't even draw a stick man."

"I was playing a part, okay? Let's go back to the hotel and regroup—seeing as Bradley didn't conveniently drop Carmen's car key, there's not a lot we can do out here until we find mine. We won't all fit in Nigel's Miata, and the security on Black's Porsche is so good that even I can't make it start without the damn key. And we need to retrieve Mack's laptop."

Mack brightened a little. "Really?"

"Really." Emmy patted her on the hand. "Me and Carmen'll go and find it while the rest of you guys tear Bradley's room apart."

CHAPTER 7

"I WANT TO know why Bradley was taken," Emmy said as they jogged back to the hotel. "I mean, who are we up against here?"

"Have you pissed anyone off lately?" Dan asked.

"Too many people to count." Emmy glanced at Nigel, who'd tagged onto the back of their group. "But for various reasons, most of them aren't able to be with us tonight. How about the rest of you?"

"Same," Carmen said.

Dan shrugged. "Most of them are in jail, unless you count cops. I've trodden on a lot of tactical-booted toes in the last year."

"I found a new way of hiding my IP address," Mack said, tossing her mane of red hair over her shoulder. She had a spring in her step that had been missing since they arrived at Cedar Ridge. "So it's not because of me."

"Bradley got in an argument at Bloomingdale's last week over the last pair of Valentino palazzo pants," Tia offered.

"Why? I've never even seen him wear palazzo pants."

"They were for you."

"I don't wear them either."

"Apparently you do now."

"Good grief." At least Emmy would have somewhere to hide her knife. "So he won the argument?"

"Of course. Bradley can out-shop anyone."

"Do you know who the fight was with?"

Tia shook her head. "Some blonde woman. There was a bunch of shouting, then he distracted her with an asymmetrical skirt and ran."

"Kidnapping seems like a drastic response."

A small voice came from the back. "I think I might know who took him."

Six heads swivelled to stare at Nigel.

"I thought you said you didn't get a good look at the men?" Emmy said.

"I didn't. But I've got an awful feeling they were here to take me instead."

The group reached the hotel, and Emmy put a finger to her lips as they tiptoed past the main reception desk. Then she paused to cast fresh eyes over Nigel. He was younger—twenty-one or twenty-two to Bradley's twenty-nine—and in daylight, there was no way his round face could be mistaken for Bradley's high cheekbones. But they shared the same build, and Bradley had dyed his hair a similar shade of blond to Nigel's a few days before they came to Cedar Ridge. In the dark? Yes, a case of mistaken identity was possible.

Emmy used the pair of bobby pins holding her hair back to make short work of the lock on Bradley's room, and once everyone got inside, she pushed the door closed behind them and pointed at the chair by the window.

"Sit," she instructed Nigel.

He took one look at her and sat.

"So, Nigel, tell me why you think somebody wanted to kidnap you. I'm dying to hear this."

"Uh, it's a long story."

"Since Bradley's life is in danger, perhaps we could go with the executive summary for now?"

"O-o-okay, I mean, yes... I'm not sure where to start."

"From the beginning." Emmy tapped her foot. "Any time in the next five seconds is fine."

"I saw a client get murdered by her husband, and now I'm on the run from him," Nigel blurted.

As Bradley would say: Holy Stromboli.

"Yeah, I can see how that might cause a problem. Why the hell didn't you go to the police?"

"Because the local sheriff was one of the men who helped him dispose of the body."

Oh, this just got better and better.

"Does this husband have a name?"

"Sheldon Bernadino, but everyone calls him Bernie."

"Who's everyone?"

"The folks who live in Fairoaks, West Virginia." A tear leaked down Nigel's cheek, then another. "W-w-what's going to happen now?"

"First, we're going to get Bradley back, and then we'll deal with your little problem. Do you have any evidence of what Bernie did?"

Nigel gulped. "A v-v-video. I took it with my phone." The tears turned into a flood. "I should have tried to save her, but I was scared he'd kill me too."

"Good. A video's good." Emmy closed her eyes for a brief second as she firmed up all the little pieces of the plan flying around in her mind. *Bradley. Focus on*

Bradley. How did he get himself into these situations? "Carmen, you're with me. Tia, you watch Nigel. If he cries, pass him tissues. If he moves, tie him to the damn chair. Dan, Mack, and Lara—tear this room apart."

"T-t-tie me up?"

"Tia's been taking macramé lessons, and she's dying to try out her new skills. Now, the jobsworth manning the reception desk confiscated my friend's laptop—where would she have put it?"

"All the contraband goes into the manager's office."

Emmy threw her head back and laughed. "Contraband. I'll show them fucking contraband. Where's the office?"

"Take the door behind the reception desk, and it's the first on the right."

"I'll be back in...who the fuck knows? I want my damn watch as well."

Apart from the faint strains of whale music coming from somewhere, the hotel lay silent as Emmy and Carmen moved down the corridor, one on each side, alert for any movement.

"Cleaner," Emmy mouthed as they approached a corner, and they scooted past while the man's head was turned. Far easier to avoid being seen than to answer questions about their missing "uniforms."

Emmy vaulted the reception desk and heard a soft *thud* as Carmen did the same. Two seconds later, they were both through the door behind it.

First on the right. There it was, just a few metres away. Locked. No matter—it only took seconds for Emmy to get the door open. She'd had so much practice at breaking and entering over the years that the manager might as well have rolled out a welcome mat.

Inside, the spartan office looked as dull as the rest of Cedar Ridge. A glowing corner lamp revealed a miniature Zen garden on one corner of the desk, and the coat cupboard held a row of matching cream uniforms. Where was Mack's bloody laptop?

"Over here," Carmen whispered, holding back a wall hanging depicting a single banana over abstract pastel stripes.

Hmm, another door. Emmy picked the lock on that one too, then pulled it open to reveal the mother lode.

"Fuck me. That hypocritical bitch."

"*Cojeme.* Is that an Xbox?"

It was, right next to the flat-screen TV, the Nintendo dance mat, and the Surface Pro tablet.

"Yup, plus she's got a cappuccino machine. *Pinche puta.*" Emmy swore in Spanish in a nod to Carmen's Mexican roots. "And is this a polyester dress?"

Carmen pinched the fabric. "Sure feels like it."

"It's hideous. And check out these spandex leggings."

"Hey, there's our stuff."

Carmen grabbed Mack's laptop bag while Emmy picked up the box containing their watches, phones, and other miscellanea deemed inappropriate for Cedar Ridge. It took all her willpower not to grab the damn coffee machine too because boy did she need the caffeine. This promised to be a long night.

"Let's go."

Back in Bradley's room, Dan held up the Porsche key in triumph. "Got it."

"Where did he hide it?"

"In a hollowed-out copy of *Eat, Pray, Love.* And I

found our money inside a fake candle."

"Good job."

From Dan, not from Bradley. A fake candle made a terrible hiding place. Did he not remember the time he'd hidden his stash of Valium in one, forgotten, then lit it two weeks later?

Carmen handed the laptop over to Mack, and she paused to kiss the lid before powering it up and plugging a custom-built Wi-Fi dongle into the side. After she'd typed in her ridiculously long password and activated the facial recognition system, she turned to Emmy.

"We've got the laptop, we've got the car keys, and we kind of know who took Bradley, but how are we going to find him? Are we heading for Fairoaks?"

"I'm hoping we don't need to go that far."

"You have a plan?"

"Of course I have a plan." Always be prepared, remember? "You know how I gave Bradley a new pair of diamond earrings for his birthday?"

"Can't miss them. They practically blind everyone."

"Yup, and they cost me bloody thousands. Enough that I had Nate build a kinetic-energy-powered tracker into the base of each, which means I can find them if Bradley loses one. And it also means we can track down Bradley if we lose him."

A slow smile spread over Mack's face. "Brilliant. All I need is the tracking ID."

"Easy—it's nine-oh-two-one-oh, Bradley's favourite zip code."

Seconds later, Blackwood's bespoke tracking program, co-written by Mack and Nate, displayed a green dot moving steadily across the screen ten miles away, and it was Emmy's turn to grin. *Now* they were having fun.

"Ready?"

A chorus of yeses came back.

"What about me?" Tia asked. "I want to come too."

"Not today, honey. I need you to stay here and keep an eye on Nigel." And Lara too. Emmy didn't know her well enough to predict how she'd hold up in a difficult situation. "Nobody wants to waste time trying to find him if he legs it."

"You promise you'll be careful?"

Emmy gave her a quick hug. "Promise. We won't be long."

She loved Tia to bits, but if this turned nasty, Emmy wanted her well away from the action. Carmen, Dan, and Mack? They were her team. They'd worked together for so long that they could practically read each other's minds.

"Good luck."

Oh, they didn't need luck. Not when they had weapons, training, and loyalty.

"Let's go rescue Bradley."

CHAPTER 8

THERE WERE NO arguments as Emmy leapt into the driver's seat of the Porsche with Carmen beside her. Mack took her spot behind Carmen, the laptop screen glowing in front of her, while Dan took the other seat in the back. They each knew their job, and Emmy's sole purpose right now was to get them to Bradley as fast as possible.

"Take a right out the gate," Mack instructed.

The Cayenne Turbo belonged to Emmy's husband, and he'd had it tuned up to exceed the manufacturer's top speed of 170 mph. Emmy made good use of the power as they sped through the night, while Dan and Carmen assembled the equipment they'd need for the job.

"What hardware are we going with?" Dan asked. "Pistols all around?"

"*Sí*," Carmen answered. "My Korth is in the case with my rifle."

Dan opened up the lockboxes under the seats, and Emmy leaned forward far enough for Carmen to strap on her custom-made holster and load it up. Would she need any of the goodies tonight? Hopefully not, but it always paid to be ready.

"Candy bar?" Dan offered. "I found them in the door pocket."

"Yes!"

Emmy stayed focused on the road as Dan held one out for her to take a bite. A Reese's Peanut Butter Bar—just what the doctor ordered. Heaven in a mouthful.

"Getting closer," Mack said. "They're three miles ahead, moving more slowly now. I think they're on foot."

The powerful engine roared as Emmy kept her foot to the floor through country lanes. Thankfully traffic was light, but they left a few startled deer in their wake as the vehicle flew along, as well as the odour of burning rubber.

"One mile," Mack announced, and Emmy eased off on the gas to keep their approach quiet.

With half a mile to go, she found an overgrown track by the side of the wooded road and nosed the SUV down it. They'd go the rest of the way on foot, silent wraiths flitting through a moonlit night.

As they assembled outside, Mack closed her laptop lid and switched to a tracking app on her phone, the screen darkened so it only showed the bare essentials—an indicator of the terrain and Bradley's green dot.

"Good to go," she whispered.

Emmy took point as they glided through the forest, with Mack second, Dan third, and Carmen bringing up the rear. The low hoot of an owl and the occasional rustle of rabbits and deer in the bushes gave no indication of the proverbial nightmare moving through the trees, about to unleash hell on whatever lay ahead.

Sure beat an evening playing Monopoly, anyway.

According to the tracker, they'd closed the distance to fifty yards when the first voices drifted through the night, a rough West Virginia accent followed by

Bradley's higher-pitched tones.

"Pick up the fuckin' shovel and dig."

"No, I will not. My boots might get dirty."

"They're gunna get dirtier when we bury you."

"Well, I'm still not helping. This calfskin will get scuffed over my dead body."

"That can be arranged."

"You're an asshole, you know that? You've already torn my jeans—my *Versace* jeans—and my sweater's got a loose thread."

Emmy glanced behind, stifling a smirk as she saw Carmen roll her eyes in the moonlight. Bloody Bradley. Trust him to be more concerned with fashion than dying. Another thirty seconds, and Mack slipped her phone into her pocket. They didn't need it anymore.

Up ahead, Bradley and his two kidnappers were gathered in a small clearing, the space lit by a hanging lantern that cast eerie shadows as it swayed in the breeze. One man tried to pass Bradley a spade while the other pointed a gun at his head. Rather than do as instructed, Bradley had folded his arms, and Emmy knew from the set of his mouth that gun or no gun, the idiot with the spade might as well give up and dig the damn hole himself.

"It's just a fuckin' sweater," the man holding the pistol growled.

"And you're just a fuckin' pig," Bradley shot back.

"Can't we shoot him right now?"

The man with the spade shrugged. "Might as well if he won't dig the hole. Bernie just said to get rid of him."

The cock of the revolver's hammer cut through the night, but that *click* was eclipsed first by the report from Carmen's Korth, and then by the gunman's howl of agony as the revolver left his hand along with several of his fingers.

Bradley dropped into a crouch, and Emmy was pleased to see that at least some of the training she'd given him over the years had paid off. A hostage should never lie flat—it made escape far too difficult.

"Dead or alive?" Carmen asked.

Emmy took a second to consider the question. Instinct told her these men were unimportant, not to mention unprofessional. Their argument with Bradley had proven that, and thanks to the guy with the spade, Team Blackwood already knew for sure that Sheldon Bernadino was behind the abduction. They didn't need the two men to provide further information.

Then there was the fact that they'd been about to commit a murder. A cold-blooded murder, and Bradley wasn't even the man they were after. They'd have killed him, then gone back for Nigel when they realised their mistake. And who knew how many other victims these two knuckle-draggers had disposed of? Emmy didn't doubt that there were more shallow graves in the forests between here and West Virginia, sons and daughters, husbands and wives, brothers and sisters who would never be found.

Emmy brought up her own Walther P88. This wasn't the first time she'd acted as judge, jury, and executioner, and it wouldn't be the last.

"Take out the trash."

Two *bang*s, two bullets, two bodies.

And one hysterical personal assistant.

"Emmy!" Bradley shrieked. "I knew you'd come."

She only just had time to holster her gun before he threw himself into her arms and hugged her tight. The smell of his Ralph Lauren cologne threatened to make her sneeze as he buried his face in her shoulder.

"They tried to make me dig my own grave," he sobbed.

"I heard."

"And they wanted to bury me in torn pants."

"Stop thinking about it."

"I c-c-can't."

"Try. Think about redecorating the living room at Little Riverley instead."

"B-b-but you said you liked it as it was."

"A girl can change her mind, can't she? Why don't you come up with a new colour scheme while we get these bodies buried?"

"Really?"

"Here, take my jacket and sit over by the lantern. We'll be done in no time."

Bradley looked down at himself. "At least I didn't get blood on my sweater. And I suppose I might be able to repair the loose thread."

Emmy wrapped her jacket around his shoulders and led him to a fallen log.

"See, there's positive thinking." Nigel would be so proud. "We'll find you some new pants as soon as we get back to the hotel."

With Bradley sitting quietly for once, it was time for the least enjoyable task of the night. Digging. Even that boot-camp run with Günter had been less unpleasant.

"I hate burial as a disposal method," Carmen grumbled, picking up one of the spades the men had brought. "It's too labour intensive."

Emmy hefted the second spade. "The secret is to use a pre-prepared hole."

Dan snorted. "Yeah, like when you were building your house."

"You buried someone under Little Riverley?" Mack asked.

"I thought you knew about that?"

"No, you never told me."

"Oops. Well, there's a paedophile under the downstairs toilet. Means I can shit on him every morning."

Mack giggled. "I won't be able to flush without thinking of that now."

"Brings a smile to my face every time. Do me a favour, would you? Go through their pockets while me and Carmen start on this bloody grave?"

The girls took it in turns to dig a hole deep enough that passing animals wouldn't be tempted to investigate, then unceremoniously dumped the bodies into it. Filling in was easier than taking out, and half an hour later they'd finished.

"It's a bit lumpy," Bradley said.

Emmy shrugged. "Yeah, the dirt never quite fits back in. Don't worry, we'll drag some branches over the top and we're golden. Are you feeling okay?"

"I'm thinking cream for the lounge with a navy-blue feature wall. Maybe a few silver accents?"

"Sounds great. New furniture too?"

A tiny smile flickered across Bradley's lips. "I could take a look at sofas?"

Emmy offered him her elbow, and he looped his arm through hers.

"Perfect."

Chapter 9

AFTER THEY'D MOVED the kidnappers' van ten miles down the road, Emmy flicked her lighter and set fire to it before climbing back behind the wheel of the Porsche.

"Shame we didn't bring marshmallows—we could have made s'mores."

Carmen checked her watch. "It's almost two a.m. Could we find some food? All that digging gave me an appetite."

"There are plenty of snacks in the trunk," Bradley said.

"No, proper food. Carbs, cheese, something fried."

"On it," Mack said from the back seat, tapping away at her keyboard. "Okay, there's a twenty-four-hour diner six miles away. Who's up for burgers?"

Dan whooped with delight. "Me! I'm so hungry I'm about to chew my own fingers off."

Bradley shuddered, squashed into the middle between her and Mack. "Please, could we stop with the finger jokes?"

Emmy drove more sedately on the way back—well, marginally—and it wasn't long before they pulled into the parking lot outside an old railway carriage, now converted into "Benny's." Inside, a waitress with the sallow complexion of a heavy smoker eyed up Bradley's silver cowboy boots and raised an eyebrow. When Emmy glared, the woman quickly averted her gaze and took out her order pad. Emmy and her friends were allowed to joke about Bradley's outrageous outfits, but nobody else was.

"Five cheeseburgers with everything," she said. "Extra fries, and keep the coffee coming."

"You won't sleep tonight," Bradley warned as they slid into a booth.

"I wasn't planning to. We've still got work to do once we get back to Cedar Ridge. Somebody needs to deal with Bernie."

"You know who he is? The two oafs kept mentioning his name, but I had no idea what they were talking about."

"I wouldn't expect you to. They were meant to kidnap the life coach from Cedar Ridge, not you."

"Nigel?"

"Yes, Nigel."

"What did Nigel do? I liked him. We had a wonderful chat about colour wheels this morning."

"It's not what he did, it's what he saw. Nigel witnessed Bernie kill his own wife, and somehow Bernie found out."

Bradley gasped in shock. "A lady died? So what was Nigel doing at Cedar Ridge? Hiding?"

"We don't have the full story yet. Nigel stayed with Tia and Lara while we came to get you."

"Ooh, ooh, we need to find out everything. Eat, eat! Quickly! I'll order three extra bags of food to go."

By the time Team Blackwood pulled back into the parking lot next to Carmen's G-Wagen, the Porsche smelled like a fast-food restaurant and nobody could eat another thing. That didn't stop Emmy from retrieving the duffel bag full of snacks and her precious coffee sachets from the Mercedes before they headed back to the main building, though.

"It's for breakfast," she explained. "That avocado mush I ate yesterday morning tasted disgusting."

"Good plan," Dan said. "Need a hand carrying anything?"

Tia's eyes lit up when they all trooped into Bradley's room and she smelled the food. "Fries? You brought fries?"

"Yup." Emmy held out a bag to her. "And we got Bradley back."

"Well, that was a given. I knew you'd get Bradley back, but the fries... That's the icing on the cake."

Great, now Emmy wanted cake as well. She jerked a thumb at Nigel, still sitting in the same chair they'd left him in.

"Did he behave?"

"He hasn't moved."

Nigel took in the newcomers, and a little of the tension seeped out of his body when he spotted Bradley at the back. Emmy saw it in the slight drop of his shoulders and a relaxing of the lines that criss-crossed his forehead.

"I didn't think you'd manage to rescue him. Bernie's men can be brutal."

"Turned out to be easy. They left Bradley tied up in this little shack in the woods, so all we had to do was cut him loose."

"But how did you even find him?"

Bradley glanced up from the Snickers bar he'd just bitten into. "Yeah, how did you find me?"

Emmy tapped the side of her nose. "Trade secret." Those earrings stayed. She'd weld them onto his ears if necessary. "Now, Nigel, you need to tell us the full story. Here, have a cheeseburger."

Nigel shook his head and pushed the food away. "I can't eat, not until this is over. I feel sick."

"Fine. Just speak."

Emmy dragged a chair over, arranging it so she sat opposite Nigel. Putting herself on the same level as an interviewee always built rapport.

He took a deep breath, knuckles white on the arms of his own chair. "It started almost a year ago when Mrs. Bernadino called me for a consultation. She'd been really stressed, and she thought that maybe I could teach her how to relax. But when we talked things through and discussed what she wanted from her life, it turned out that her only wish was to leave her husband."

"And I take it he wasn't too happy about that?"

Nigel's hair flopped over one eye as he shook his head. "She always said he'd kill her if he found out. He was a monster, a control freak, and he kept her locked in the house most of the time. Oh, he'd pay for anything she wanted—clothes, shoes, jewellery, weekly visits from a stylist, a personal masseuse, art lessons—but that was no substitute for love. All she wanted was her freedom."

"Why did she marry him in the first place?"

"The whole cliché—Sheldon Bernadino was a forty-year-old charmer who snared a girl half his age from a terrible part of town with promises of everything she could dream of. She saw his true colours when he... when he raped her on their wedding night."

Nigel began sniffing, and Bradley passed over a handful of tissues.

"Since when is that a discussion a person has with a life coach?"

"We became friends, okay? Neither of us had many."

"You liked her, didn't you? As more than just a client?"

His tears fell harder. "Yeah, I did like Lorella, but nothing happened, I swear. Neither of us would have dared with Mr. Bernadino around."

"But she asked you to help her escape?"

"Not asked. I offered. If you'd seen the way she was living, the bruises all over her, you couldn't have left her there either."

"So what went wrong?"

"Mr. Bernadino held a weekly poker game, him and a few buddies. They'd sit in his den and get drunk for hours, and I'd sneak in and talk to Lorella. Until that night, he'd never come upstairs earlier than two o'clock in the morning, but...but..."

Nigel gulped for air, and Lara settled an arm around his shoulders. "It's okay. I know it's difficult."

"Did he finish the game early?" Emmy asked.

"No, the sick bastard bet her as part of a losing hand."

"He what?"

Nigel's voice dropped to a whisper. "He ran out of chips, so he bet a night with his wife instead."

"Fuck me."

"We heard them coming, and I hid in the closet. She fought back. She fought back, but Mr. Bernadino held her down while his friend raped her, and when they'd finished, she wasn't breathing anymore. His hands were around her *neck*."

"Bernadino's hands?"

"Yes."

"Did he try to resuscitate her? Call an ambulance?"

Nigel shook his head. "He just said the relationship had run its course. *Run its course.* As if they'd grown apart or something. I nearly threw up right there in the closet."

"That's cold."

"The man's a monster, a psychopathic monster. He treated Lorella like a possession. A pet he expected to obey him. After she died, he dumped her body into a garbage bag."

"And you got this on camera?"

Nigel nodded, clinging to Lara's hand for support. "I should have tried to stop them, but I was scared, and...and..."

"And you'd have been dead too. How does the sheriff fit in with this?"

"He was playing poker with Mr. Bernadino. All of the players helped to bury the body afterwards."

What happened to upholding the damn law?

"Do you know where?"

"Not the exact spot, but it was somewhere behind the house. They were all too drunk to drive anywhere. That's the only reason I got away. One of them spotted me running down the road to my car, but when they chased after me in Mr. Bernadino's BMW, they crashed into a tree."

"And how did you end up here?"

Because surely nobody would choose to come to Cedar Ridge voluntarily?

"Just kept driving until I ran out of gas. I only had fifty bucks in my wallet, but when I stopped to fill up and buy food, I saw an advert for a job here in the local paper. It seemed perfect. No phones, no email, no cameras. I didn't think they'd find me."

"You can find anyone if you look hard enough."

That was a fact everyone in the room knew all too well. Sometimes it took time, often it took money, but perseverance always paid off.

"I realise that now. But I didn't have anywhere else to go, so I slept in my car until I'd earned enough to rent a room in town. Now I'll have to leave again, won't I?"

"Yeah, you will, at least until we can get Bernie arrested and the Fairoaks Sheriff's Department cleaned out."

Nigel looked up at Emmy, wiping his cheeks. "What do you mean? You're going to help me?"

"No one can kill an innocent woman, then kidnap my assistant, and expect to get away with it. Of course we're going to help you. Now, eat the damn cheeseburger because fainting from hunger isn't going to improve matters."

CHAPTER 10

EMMY LEANED BACK in the chair and sighed. Yes, a long night was about to get even longer.

"Tia, Lara, you need to go to bed. And you, Bradley."

"I'm not tired," Tia said.

"I don't care, and it's not optional."

"But—"

"No buts."

The next part of the impromptu job would be the most unpleasant, but watching Nigel's video was unfortunately necessary. Emmy needed to check his side of the story. Lara slipped out of the door without a murmur, but Tia still managed a dirty look as she stomped back to her room. She hated being left out of anything, even though she had to know Emmy only did it to protect her.

Bradley paused to give Emmy a hug before he left.

"Thanks, boss," he whispered.

"Any time, rock star."

Once he and his sparkly boots had gone, Mack set her laptop up on the desk.

"Where's the video?" she asked Nigel. "Tell me you didn't leave it on your phone?"

"No, I was scared they could make it disappear forever, so I uploaded a copy to a file-hosting service."

She spun the keyboard towards him. "Here, log in."

A minute later, a surprisingly clear picture appeared frozen on the screen, showing a pretty blonde woman lying on a king-sized bed in a pale-pink silk robe. The edge of the closet door Nigel had been hiding behind formed a black line on one side of the frame.

"Mack, you go. Take Nigel into the bathroom."

"Are you sure?"

"I'll call if we need either of you."

In the past, Mack's stomach had proven overly delicate in these types of situations, and the last thing Emmy wanted to do tonight was clean vomit off the carpet. Killing a man, burying two bodies, and watching a girl get murdered was quite enough, thanks very much.

"Ready?" she asked.

Carmen and Dan both nodded, and the three gripped each other's hands as Emmy hit play.

It was every bit as bad as she'd feared. Really, there wasn't an easy way to watch a girl get raped, especially when you'd experienced the horror for yourself as Emmy had. As Lorella Bernadino struggled in vain against two men much bigger than her, Emmy's resolve hardened while her ice-cold heart melted a little, and she vowed that the two monsters carrying out the despicable acts on the screen in front of her wouldn't see out the month. Some men didn't deserve to walk this earth.

Carmen clearly felt the same way. "Which one do you want?"

"You can have Bernadino. I want to cut the other one's dick off and put it in a blender."

"Might be hard to make that look like an accident."

Emmy scrunched her lips to one side. "I know. I'll have to give it some thought."

"What about the sheriff?" Dan asked.

"The FBI can deal with him. I've got contacts in the Public Corruption program, and I'd say this falls under their remit. We can hand over the file in a few weeks. Could you see what else you can dig up in the meantime? Nine times out of ten, dirty cops aren't just grubby, they're up to their neck in sewage."

"With pleasure."

Usually, the girls sealed deals like this with their drinks of choice—Bombay Sapphire for Emmy, Patrón for Carmen, and Jack Daniels for Dan—but in the absence of a minibar, they settled for a group hug instead. Once a team, always a team.

"Mack, it's safe," Emmy called.

She led Nigel back in, and the two perched on the end of the bed.

"Have you got a plan?" Mack asked.

"Yup."

"Do I want to know it?"

"Probably not."

"What are we doing about Nigel?"

Nigel... Nigel... "How do you fancy staying near Richmond for a month or two?"

"Will it be safe?"

"As a fortress."

"Uh, I'd love to, but I won't have enough money for rent, not if I have to leave my job."

"How do you like decorating?"

"Decorating?"

"Bradley could use a hand redoing my lounge."

"I could definitely help with that. I took an interior

design course at community college."

"There we go—sorted. Now, it's time for us to get some rest before our last day in the fun factory, and if anyone tries to make me drink nettle and ginger tea for breakfast again, I'm gonna throw the damn cup."

"Where should I sleep?" Nigel asked.

"Take Dan's room. She can share with Mack."

Dan went to collect her things, and Mack saved Nigel's video to the secure network at Blackwood before she headed off for some shut-eye as well. Only Carmen stayed behind, stretched out on the bed as Emmy changed into the sportswear she habitually slept in when away from home.

"Nice shooting tonight, Dime," Emmy said.

"You too, Valkyrie. That was a great headshot."

"I was aiming for centre mass." Emmy held out a hand, and yes, there was still a definite tremor. "Caffeine withdrawal's a bitch. Do you think Bradley's right? Should I try to cut down on coffee?"

Carmen picked a stray peppermint tea sachet off the quilt and flicked it at her. "Try this?"

"I'd tell you to fuck off if you weren't probably right."

"You don't need to quit completely. Most things are good in moderation."

"Like assassination? When we arrived, I thought the whole weekend would be boring as hell, but this evening certainly livened things up."

"Who'd have thought a trip to the spa would result in so much drama?"

"You forget Bradley organised it."

"Ah, *sí*, he always finds trouble. Remember when he made us go to the beach and we ended up sunbathing in the middle of a drug-smuggling operation?"

Oh, that day had been fun—Emmy rarely got to ride on a coastguard cutter. And luckily, the drugs hadn't belonged to Eduardo. She didn't condone those particular activities of his, but he was gradually getting out of the drug trade, and if the DEA had to bust someone, she was thankful it hadn't been the man she thought of as a father.

"How could I forget? Bradley makes life so much more colourful."

Carmen levered herself off the bed. "We all love him really."

The girls exchanged one final hug before Emmy fought against her inevitable nightmares.

"Yes, we do."

CHAPTER 11

BRADLEY ELBOWED EMMY in the ribs at the breakfast table the next morning, eyes wide.

"Sweet Mary Jane, she's coming this way."

Emmy peered over the rim of her coffee cup as the manager strode in their direction, her eyes locked onto Mack's tablet, which was sitting next to her on the table. Or was she looking at Bradley's diamanté-covered neon-green skinny jeans? Or Tia's sequined top? They'd all made an effort to dress up for breakfast, and Bradley's cowboy boots had gotten another outing just to make him even more sparkly.

"Where are your tunics?" she hissed. "And is that an electronic device?"

"Our tunics got arrested for crimes against fashion," Tia explained.

Before the woman could hook her barbs into Tia, Carmen cut in. "Yes, it's an iPad. Probably you wouldn't recognise it since you seem to be more of a Microsoft fan."

"I beg your pardon?" The woman leaned towards Emmy and sniffed. "Is that coffee you're drinking?"

"Sure is. I figured you wouldn't mind since you're fond of a cappuccino yourself. Perhaps you wouldn't mind making me one with the fancy machine in your office?"

Map

The woman paled a shade. "How do you know about that?"

"Oh, just a rumour, but thanks for confirming it."

"I can't have guests acting like this at Cedar Ridge."

"And I can't listen to a hypocrite preaching about the evils of modern technology when she spends her lunch breaks playing *Grand Theft Auto*."

Especially when it wasn't nearly as much fun as the real thing.

"That's it! You need to leave right now."

Emmy checked her watch. "We're paid up for another six hours and forty-five minutes. Don't worry, we'll be hightailing it out of here at four on the dot."

"Don't even consider coming back."

The entire table burst into laughter, and diners who'd been pretending to look away turned and stared openly.

"Don't worry, love. If we find ourselves with time to kill in the future, there are plenty of other places where we can do it."

"Today didn't turn out so bad, did it?" Mack said as they lifted the last of their luggage into the cars. Between the eight of them, they'd made light work of carrying everything to the parking lot.

"That masseur certainly worked my kinks out," Dan said, grinning. "All of them."

"Oh, Dan, you didn't?"

"Of course I did. He was hot."

"Aren't you ever going to settle down?"

"I'm not planning to."

"I bet you will one day. You'll meet your Luke."

"I hope not—I only understand half of what Luke says. Most of the time he speaks in techno-jargon."

Emmy felt the same way as Dan, but Mack's eyes took on a dreamy look. "I love that about him."

Oh, please, spare the saccharine. Emmy slammed the boot of the Porsche closed.

"Ready to go? Nigel, are you sure you've got everything?"

"Yes. I kept all my stuff in my car just in case I needed to run again."

"And you've got the address in case you get left behind?"

"In my satnav."

"Great. Let's ship out."

Emmy wouldn't be sorry to see the back of Cedar Ridge. How people could stay there voluntarily was beyond her, and the manager was a real piece of work. The holistic equivalent of a vegetarian who ate bacon for brunch, or a climate activist who drove a Dodge Ram on the weekends, or a fitness guru who had liposuction... But before Emmy could hop into the driver's seat, her phone rang with Alannah Myles's "Black Velvet," chosen because of the way her husband's fingers slid down her thighs and... *Stop it, Emmy. Just answer the damn phone.*

"Diamond, I missed you."

Now who was being sweet? "Missed you too, Mr. Black. How's Vegas?"

"We're about to fly back."

"Did you have a good time? A wild weekend of gambling and strip shows?"

"Not exactly."

"So it was boring?"

How could Vegas be boring?

"Oh, there was one interesting part. You'll never guess what happened…"

EPILOGUE

FROM THE *FAIROAKS Observer*, June 24th

Local businessman Sheldon Bernadino's life was cut devastatingly short in what is believed to be an out-of-season hunting accident last weekend. Mr. Bernadino mentioned his intention to bag a deer to several acquaintances, and when he didn't show up at his weekly poker game, they raised the alarm. Law enforcement officials found him with a fatal head wound in the woods behind his house, but as yet, they have no leads on the culprit. Anyone with information is asked to contact the sheriff's department.

"It was only a matter of time before something like this happened," a local resident told the Observer. *"Too many people out hunting early this year. Rich folks think the law doesn't apply to them."*

The death is the second tragedy to hit the Bernadino family this year, following the unsolved disappearance of Sheldon's wife, Lorella. Close friends are said to be shocked at the news.

Mr. Bernadino's funeral will be held at 2 p.m. on June 30th at Our Lady of Peace Chapel.

From the *Fairoaks Observer*, June 29th

Following on from the devastating loss of one of its most prominent citizens last week, Fairoaks has been dealt another blow with the death of Paul Wesser, of the town's law firm Wesser & Phillips. Mr. Wesser slipped while attempting to prune a cedar tree in his backyard with a chainsaw, and the resulting damage to the femoral artery and surrounding tissue meant his death was sadly inevitable.

We at the Fairoaks Observer *would like to remind all budding gardeners to follow proper safety procedures and to consider using a professional for the trickier jobs. Take a look at our landscaping feature on page 37, which includes a list of certified arborists in the local area.*

WHAT'S NEXT?

So, what *did* happen in Vegas? The Blackwood Security series continues in Out of the Blue...

Chess Lane is getting married. The church is booked, the guests are invited, and in three short weeks her husband will give her a night she'll never forget. Only her wedding happens a little sooner than she planned when she meets Jed Harker, a CIA agent with a big ego and a bigger... No, she doesn't even want to think about it.

Chess has hit rock bottom when a simple favour for a colleague leads her to Washington, DC and an offer she can't refuse. As chaos spreads faster than the plague, one thing's for sure—her life will never be the same again. But will anybody else's?

Find out more here: www.elise-noble.com/blue

If you enjoyed Neon, please consider leaving a review.

For an author, every review is incredibly important. Not only do they make us feel warm and fuzzy inside, readers consider them when making their decision whether or not to buy a book. Even a line saying you enjoyed the book or what your favourite part was helps a lot.

Want to Stalk Me?

For updates on my new releases, giveaways, and other random stuff, you can sign up for my newsletter on my website:
www.elise-noble.com

Facebook:
www.facebook.com/EliseNobleAuthor

Twitter: @EliseANoble

Instagram: @elise_noble

If you're on Facebook, you may also like to join Team Blackwood for exclusive giveaways, sneak previews, and book-related chat. Be the first to find out about new stories, and you might even see your name or one of your ideas make it into print!

And if you'd like to read my books for FREE, you can also find details of how to join my advance review team.

Would you like to join Team Blackwood?

www.elise-noble.com/team-blackwood

End of Book Stuff

When I first introduced Bradley in Pitch Black, I knew I wanted to write a story about him, but as he's happily settled with Miles, I didn't have enough for a full novel. But when Bradley's around, there's always drama, so I figured it was only natural he'd run into trouble organising Mack's bachelorette party. He has a few problems at the wedding too, but you can read about that in Out of the Blue. And I'm sure he'll cause more havoc in future :)

Big thanks to my lovely friend Rach who did the first read through this story in the pub one lunchtime (The Blackwood Arms, where else?)—when she kept laughing, I knew I'd got something right.

And thanks to my Team Blackwood beta readers: Chandni, Hence, Jeff, Erazm, Helen, Terri, and Musi. Plus my wonderful editor, Amanda, and my proof readers, Emma, John, and Dominique. I might write the stories, but these books wouldn't be what they are without your help.

Other Books by Elise Noble

The Blackwood Security Series
For the Love of Animals (Nate & Carmen - prequel)
Black is My Heart (Diamond & Snow - prequel)
Pitch Black
Into the Black
Forever Black
Gold Rush
Gray is My Heart
Neon (novella)
Out of the Blue
Ultraviolet
Glitter (novella)
Red Alert
White Hot
Sphere (novella)
The Scarlet Affair
Spirit (novella)
Quicksilver
The Girl with the Emerald Ring
Red After Dark
When the Shadows Fall (2020)

The Blackwood Elements Series
Oxygen
Lithium

Carbon
Rhodium
Platinum
Lead
Copper
Bronze
Nickel
Hydrogen (TBA)

The Blackwood UK Series
Joker in the Pack
Cherry on Top (novella)
Roses are Dead
Shallow Graves
Indigo Rain
Pass the Parcel (TBA)

Blackwood Casefiles
Stolen Hearts
Burning Love (TBA)

Blackstone House
Hard Lines (2021)
Hard Tide (TBA)

The Electi Series
Cursed
Spooked
Possessed
Demented
Judged (2021)

The Planes Series

A Vampire in Vegas (2021)

The Trouble Series
Trouble in Paradise
Nothing but Trouble
24 Hours of Trouble

Standalone
Life
Coco du Ciel (2021)
Twisted (short stories)
A Very Happy Christmas (novella)

Books with clean versions available (no swearing and no on-the-page sex)
Pitch Black
Into the Black
Forever Black
Gold Rush
Gray is My Heart

Audiobooks
Black is My Heart (Diamond & Snow - prequel)
Pitch Black
Into the Black
Forever Black
Gold Rush
Gray is My Heart